The Christmas Star

To Sheila for her love of Christmas and stories
and Marvin for his love of gardening.
Thank you for pointing me in the right direction.
-Jamin

ISBN 13: 978-1-4621-3588-2

Published by CFI, an imprint of Cedar Fort, Inc.
2373 W. 700 S., Springville, UT 84663
Distributed by Cedar Fort, Inc., www.cedarfort.com

Library of Congress Control Number: 2020945608

Cover design and typesetting by Shawnda T. Craig

Printed in the United States of America

10 9 8 7 6 5 4 3 2 1

Printed on acid-free paper

written by Jamin Bingham • illustrated by Andres Balcazar

CFI • An imprint of Cedar Fort, Inc. • Springville, Utah

In Heaven, every angel has a job.
Some angels sing, and some deliver messages, but my job is the best of all. I am a gardener, and I raise stars.

The garden is full of star trees, but each one seems to have its own personality. Each tree varies in size and color and is as unique as the stars on it.

At night, the stars on the trees fill the entire garden with heavenly light. Sometimes I find myself standing there, breathing in the sweet scent of star blossoms, amazed at the beauty around me.

This year was special.

One star grew bigger and brighter than the rest. This star would be a sign to the world that Jesus was born.

I had to make sure it had plenty of sunlight, heat, and stardust. I read stories to it and would tell it what a special star it was. It continued to grow bigger and brighter.

Hearing the news that Mary and Joseph were leaving for Bethlehem made everyone so excited.

The air was ringing with sounds
of heavenly choirs practicing.

I looked at my star and smiled. It was flawless.
I plucked it and placed it in a case with clouds for padding.

This was it.

Reaching Bethlehem, I found a large palace and went inside to find Mary and Joseph. The palace was beautiful, certainly fit for a king.

I did not find Mary and Joseph anywhere. I even searched the servants' quarters, where I found a little child. She was sitting in a dark corner crying, cold and afraid.

Without thinking, I opened the star's case and broke off one golden point. It lit up the room, and the child's eyes sparkled. She gave me a crooked little smile.

I wiped the tears from her cheeks and took out the cloud I had used to carefully pack the star. Flattening it out into a blanket, I tucked it gently around her.

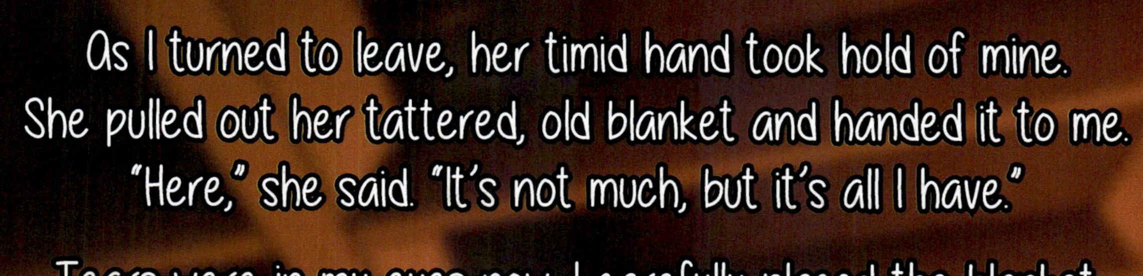

As I turned to leave, her timid hand took hold of mine. She pulled out her tattered, old blanket and handed it to me. "Here," she said. "It's not much, but it's all I have."

Tears were in my eyes now. I carefully placed the blanket around the star. "Thank you," I replied, smiling.

As I left, I realized what I had done.

I wanted to cry out, "I didn't mean to give that to you. Please give it back!" but the memory of her smile stopped me, and I continued on.

Leaving the palace, I wasn't sure where to go. I knew Mary and Joseph were coming to Bethlehem, but where? It was getting dark. That's when I noticed a young shepherd boy looking as distraught as I felt.

I asked him what was wrong, and he said he was missing one of his sheep. If he didn't find it soon, a wolf might get it. "I don't know how I will ever find it now," he said in despair.

My star's light could help.

Losing one more point might make it look more even. I reached into the case and pulled free another piece. Handing it to the shepherd boy, I said, "This light will guide you to your lost sheep."

"Thank you," he responded with wide eyes. Before I left, he asked me where I was going. I told him I was looking for someone visiting Bethlehem. "You might try an inn," he said. I thanked him and hurried off.

I searched inn after inn.

The night grew darker. Mary and Joseph were nowhere. I kept searching though. That's when I noticed a family huddled in an alleyway.

They looked tired and cold. The inns were all full, and the father didn't know how to keep his family warm.

I opened my case, broke off another golden point, and handed it to him. The warmth filled the alley.

I quickly walked away.

I couldn't find the Christ child, and I felt so ashamed. Even if I did find Him, what could I do? My star was ruined. It was no longer suitable to mark His birthplace.

When I got to the edge of town, I found a small building and hid behind it. All I could do was sit and cry.

Opening the case, I peered inside. My star was dull, and all but the bottom point was gone. I hung my head in shame. Such a perfect star—broken.

I decided to hang the star anyway.

I looked at the quiet building and noticed it was a stable. I knew nobody would look for the star here, so I hung it in the empty sky above the stable.

The sky grew bright. Looking up, I saw my star glowing. It lit the entire sky. I stood there confused, shaking my head. My star had been broken and battered

As I sat there gazing up, I heard a tiny noise. Around the corner was a beautiful young woman holding a newborn infant in her arms.

Looking at the child, my heart caught fire. I dropped to my knees. It was Jesus! Nothing was too broken for Him to fix. The star was perfect, because it was His.

I reached into my case, pulled out the little blanket, and handed it to Mary. I repeated the little girl's words: "Here. It's not much, but it's all I have." Mary smiled as she wrapped her child.

The heavens opened,
and choirs of angels
filled the air.

The last remaining tip of the
star pointed down like
an arrow from heaven,
marking Christ's birthplace.

I finally understood. He was not born at a palace or an inn. He, the Creator of the world, was born in a stable.

"And she brought forth her firstborn son, and wrapped him in swaddling clothes, and laid him in a manger." (Luke 2:7)